I'm a Potty Champion!

By Kitty Higgins
Illustrated by John Nez

BARRON'S

How to Properly Use
I'm a Potty Champion!
Book and Trophy

It is important to note that each child's development is unique—potty-training ranges from ages two to four. We suggest that parents read this book to their child two to three times to introduce the idea of potty-training. Each parent will also have to decide, based upon each child's level of language understanding, when it is appropriate to introduce this book. Once the concept of potty-training is familiar to the child, the parent can then bring in the potty chair, explain to the child its purpose, and show the child its location in the bathroom.

Parents may introduce the concept of the trophy as an incentive and place it in an area where the child can view it but cannot reach it. For example, the trophy can be placed on top of the refrigerator, where the child can see it and is reminded that it will one day be his or hers.

It is up to the parents to decide when the potty chair has been used "properly" (see page 11). Once your child has success using the potty chair, it is time to reward him or her with the trophy. By using the enclosed stickers, a parent can personalize the trophy by spelling the child's name across the bottom of the trophy. At that point, parents can give the child the trophy and declare that he or she is truly a potty champion. The trophy should be the first of many encouraging words praising your child for using the potty!

—*Kitty Higgins and
Dr. Ray Cardwell*

I am a potty champion, you can be one, too!
Read the next few pages, I'll show you what to do.

One day Mom came home from shopping with a very big box. She opened it and said, "This is a potty chair just for you!"

She put the potty chair in the bathroom, between the toilet and the tub. Next to the potty she put a basket with some toys and my favorite books.

Mom sat me down on the potty chair. She said, "This is where you pee and poop. If you sit here a few times each day, soon you'll see how easy it is."

The first day I sat on the potty and read all my
books but nothing happened.

The next day I played with
Teddy but still nothing happened.

The day after that, I didn't want to sit on the potty chair. Mom said, "That's okay, we will try again tomorrow."

Every day I'd sit and sit. Mom would bring me a
different book or toy to play with, but when we'd
look in the potty, nothing had happened.

One afternoon, Teddy and I were coloring. Something funny in my tummy told me that I should sit on the potty! I did, and I went pee! I was so excited that I called to Mom and Dad.

"Come and see! Look at this!" And they all
looked with amazement at what I had done.

Mom went to call Grandma. Dad emptied the potty into the toilet, and I got to flush it myself!

Mom hugged me and Dad said, "You're a potty champion." He handed me a trophy.
"Wow!" I said, "I'm a potty champion!"

The next afternoon Teddy and I went outside to play. I took him for a ride in my wagon.

My tummy felt kind of funny and
I said to Teddy, "I think I'd better go in."
But we were having such a good time, I didn't.
I pooped in my pants!

I cried while Mom helped me change my pants.
Then she gave Teddy and me a glass of milk
and a cookie and sat with us. She said, "Do you
know what? I think Dad and I forgot to tell you
what it really means to be a potty champion...

"A potty champion is someone who tries to pee and poop in the potty chair every day. A potty champion is also someone who forgets sometimes, and has an accident. But most of all, this potty champion is the one who Dad and I love, and the one who we know will, some day soon, use the potty every day."

When Dad came home, he had a package under his arm. "These are for you," he said. He held up a new pair of training underwear.

I'm a Potty Champion,
You can be one, too!
Just try every day,
Soon it will be easy for you.